HEIDI HECKELBECK

and the Wacky Tacky Spirit Week

By Wanda Coven
Illustrated by Priscilla Burris

LITTLE SIMON

New York London Toronto Sydney New Delhi

LITTLE SIMON

An imprint of Simon & Schuster Children's Publishing Division

1230 Avenue of the Americas, New York, New York 10020

First Little Simon paperback edition September 2019

Copyright © 2019 by Simon & Schuster, Inc.

Also available in a Little Simon hardcover edition.

All rights reserved, including the right of reproduction in whole or in part in any form.

LITTLE SIMON is a registered trademark of Simon & Schuster, Inc., and associated colophon is a trademark of Simon & Schuster, Inc.

For information about special discounts for bulk purchases, please contact Simon & Schuster Special Sales at 1-866-506-1949 or business@simonandschuster.com.

The Simon & Schuster Speakers Bureau can bring authors to your live event. For more information or to book an event contact the Simon & Schuster Speakers Bureau at 1-866-248-3049 or visit our website at www.simonspeakers.com.

Designed by Ciara Gay

Manufactured in the United States of America 0719 MTN

10 9 8 7 6 5 4 3 2 1

Library of Congress Cataloging-in-Publication Data

Names: Coven, Wanda, author. | Burris, Priscilla, illustrator.

Title: Heidi Heckelbeck and the wacky tacky Spirit Week / by Wanda Coven ; illustrated by Priscilla Burris.

Description: First Little Simon paperback edition. | New York : Little Simon, 2019. | Series: Heidi Heckelbeck ; [27] | Summary: Everything Heidi tries to do for Spirit Week at school seems to be wrong, at least according to her nemesis, Melanie, until a spell helps her find her superpower on Super Hero Thursday.

Identifiers: LCCN 2018052799 | ISBN 9781534446359 (pbk) | ISBN 9781534446366 (hc) | ISBN 9781534446373 (eBook)

Subjects: | CYAC: Schools—Fiction. | Conduct of life—Fiction. | Witches—Fiction.

Classification: LCC PZ7.C83393 Hbv 2019 | DDC [Fic] —dc23

LC record available at https://lccn.loc.gov/2018052799

CONTENTS

Chapter 1

THiNG-A-MA-BOBS

Heidi Heckelbeck handed a brown paper bag to her little brother. She had written his name, Henry Heckelbeck, on it.

"You can put YOUR thing-a-ma-bobs in here," she said. "And I'll put MY thing-a-ma-bobs in this bag."

Henry wrinkled his brow. "Okay. But I have one question. What's a THINK-a-ma-bob?"

Heidi sighed loudly. "The word is 'THING-A-MA-BOB.' They are like doohickeys and random stuff we may need for this week. Do you understand?"

"Kind of," said Henry.

Heidi looked at the clock. "Ready? On your mark. Get set. GO!"

Then Heidi and Henry took off on a wild thing-a-ma-bob hunt.

Henry ran to the desk in the kitchen and yanked open the top drawer. He stuck two rubber bands and a plastic spider in his bag.

Heidi found the leftover party favor drawer and pulled out a purple tiara.

There were also silver-and-pink beaded necklaces. Then she searched all the cupboards in the family room.

"Score!" she cried, holding up a can of unopened neon-green Silly String. She plopped it into her bag.

Her next stop was the art supply cabinet. Heidi grabbed a tube of sequins, a handful of pom-poms, and a

fistful of pipe cleaners. She had no clue how she was going to use all this stuff, but she would worry about that later.

Down the hall, Henry was busy checking the bathroom drawers. He crammed dental floss and cotton balls into his bag.

Meanwhile, Heidi headed all the way up to the attic. She opened a tub of Christmas decorations. *There have to be good thing-a-ma-bobs in here,* she thought.

Heidi pulled out a tinsel garland and wound it around her neck like a sparkly boa. Then she thumpity-thumped downstairs to the kitchen.

Henry had jammed an empty box of Chocolate Oaty-O's on his head.

"What do you think of my hat?" he asked.

Heidi giggled. "I think it's CRUMBY. Get it? Cereal? Crumbs?"

Henry rolled his eyes. "I'm supposed to be a cereal BOX-er."

He punched the air with his fists.

"*I* get it!" Dad said, air-boxing as he walked into the room with Mom.

"Well, I don't get it at all," said Mom. "What in the world are you guys up to?"

Heidi and Henry looked at their mom like this was the silliest question on the planet.

"You mean you don't KNOW about this week?" Heidi asked.

Her parents shook their heads.

"Spirit Week starts tomorrow!" Heidi explained. "Each day we have to show our school spirit in different ways. It starts with Crazy Hair Day!"

Henry pranced in front of Heidi with the cereal box still on his head. "Tuesday is Silly Hat Day!"

Then Heidi bumped her brother to the side and fluffed up her boa. "Wednesday is Wacky Tacky Day!"

Across the room, Henry climbed onto a chair and struck a pose with his fists on his hips. "Can you guess what THURSDAY is?" he asked his parents.

Dad snapped his fingers. "Is it Crazy Kids Standing on the Furniture Day?"

"Nope! It's SUPERHERO Day!" Henry cheered. Then he jumped off the chair and pretended to fly.

"I hope Friday is *Normal Day*," Mom said.

Heidi shook her head. "Friday is the FUND RUN! Students run as many laps around the track as they can, and their friends and family donate money to the school for each lap."

Dad put his arm around Mom.

"Well, is there anything we can do to help?"

Heidi and Henry shot each other a look.

"YES!" Heidi cried. "Can you help us DYE our hair?"

Chapter 2

PURPLE STREAK

Heidi and Henry couldn't wait to go to school on Crazy Hair Day.

Henry had lime-green hair with a Silly String spiderweb on top. Mom had even clipped a plastic spider to the web.

It looked crazy!

Heidi worried that Henry might have gone a bit *too* crazy with his hairdo. She had decided to put one purple streak in her hair. That felt like the right amount of crazy to her.

"Swag on!" Heidi said. Then she snapped her fingers and swaggered out the back door.

But Heidi lost her swag when she got to the bus stop. Everyone had incredibly crazy hair. Bryce Beltran had teased her hair up high and given it white stripes to look like a total glamour ghoul.

"Wow!" Henry exclaimed. "You look frightful!"

Bryce twirled around.

"Thanks," she said. "I love yours, too!" Then she turned to Heidi. "How come you didn't do anything for Crazy Hair Day?"

Heidi pointed to her purple streak, and Bryce squinted as if the streak were hard to see.

"It's different," Bryce said, "but it's not exactly CRAZY."

Heidi's face flushed as she got on the bus. There were fantastic hairdos in every row.

One boy had a Mohawk. Eve Etsy had a pink wig with curlers, and Natalie Newman had pigtail braids that tied together!

Heidi sat next to her friend Bruce Bickerson and stared in wonder. He had electrified hair, like a mad scientist. He also wore safety goggles and a lab coat with little clouds puffing out.

"I used cotton balls to make the clouds," Bruce said excitedly. "They make it look like an experiment gone bad. Do you like it?"

Heidi nodded glumly and said, "It's great."

Then Bruce nudged Heidi with his elbow. "SUPERCOOL purple streak!" he said.

Heidi looked up and smiled. "You really think so?"

"Totally!" Bruce said. "Not everyone has to go bonkers on Crazy Hair Day!"

Heidi looked out the window. She sure hoped Bruce was right.

Chapter 3

NOT TOO CRAZY

Heidi's hope fizzled when she arrived at school. *Everybody* had crazier hair than Heidi.

As she stepped into the crowd, somebody mysterious tapped Heidi on the shoulder. It was her best friend Lucy Lancaster.

Her hair was swirled in a bun and bejeweled with tiny pearls. She looked like a queen.

"You look STUNNING," Heidi said with a happy gasp.

"You look great too!" Lucy said.

Heidi smiled and looked away. Bruce didn't even have a chance to respond. He had a crazy hair fan club forming around him.

Lucy grabbed Heidi by the hand. "Come on! We should go check out everyone's crazy hairstyles!"

They found Stanley Stonewrecker. He had dyed his hair green and put plastic dinosaurs and trees in it.

"He has an ancient forest on his head!" Lucy cried. Stanley waved at Heidi and Lucy.

"Check out Mr. Doodlebee!" Heidi said, pointing at their art teacher. "He has an OCTOPUS on his head!" The girls giggled. Mr. Doodlebee had a bun on top of his head with two googly eyes on it. The rest of his long hair had been braided to look like tentacles.

Heidi elbowed Lucy as Melanie
Maplethorpe pranced up to the girls
and spun around.

"*Neigh!*" Melanie announced. "Can
you guess what I
am?"

Melanie's hair
had been styled
with a horn in
front and a mane
in the back.
She had woven
rainbow ribbons
into her hair to
complete her look.

"Wow, Melanie," Heidi said. "Your hair looks MAGICAL."

"That's because I am a unicorn!" Melanie smiled. "And it looks like you have only a *tiny* streak of school spirit, Heidi. Maybe you should try a little harder tomorrow."

Heidi frowned as Melanie trotted off.

"Hmm. Why did I just say something so nice to that mean unicorn?" Heidi mumbled.

Lucy gave a shrug. "Well, her hair *was* kind of amazing."

Heidi scowled because she knew this was true. "Merg!" she grumbled. It was going to be a very hairy day.

Chapter 4

SODA POP TOP

THUD! Heidi dropped her backpack to the floor. Next she kicked off her sneakers, which bounced off the wall. *Kabonk! Kabonk!* Then she stomped into the kitchen and slammed open a cabinet looking for food.

"What's all the ruckus?" asked Dad.

33

Heidi folded her arms. "I'M all the ruckus, okay?"

Dad didn't react. Instead, he opened the cupboard and pulled out cocoa packets and two mugs.

"Have a seat," he said. "I was just about to make some cocoa."

He emptied the packets into the mugs, poured warm water on top, and stirred. Heidi sat down.

Dad slid a mug in front of his daughter. "So, what's up?"

Heidi stuck a finger in her cocoa and licked it.

"I had a yucky day," she admitted. "My crazy hair was Blahsville, USA."

Dad listened and sipped his drink slowly. Then he asked, "What's tomorrow's theme?"

Heidi sighed. "It's Crazy Hat Day, and I haven't thought of anything."

Dad set his mug on the table and got up. "I have an idea," he said, and zipped into the family room.

After searching through several bookshelves, he came back with an old photo album. Then he pulled his chair close to Heidi's.

"These are pictures of me from before you were born," Dad said.

He opened the album and flipped through the pages.

"Your hair was so LONG!" Heidi exclaimed with a laugh.

"Got you to smile!" Dad said.

They looked at pictures of Dad from cradle to college. Then Dad found the picture he'd been looking for. "This is me on *my* Crazy Hat Day."

Heidi leaned closer to get a better look. Dad had a soda bottle and a plastic cup on top of his head. His hair was the soda pouring into the cup.

Heidi turned to her dad. "I WANT TO DO THAT!"

Dad smiled. "I was hoping you'd like it," he said, "because I can help. All we need is an empty soda bottle, an empty cup, a ponytail tie, and a hair clip."

Heidi and her father raced off to collect all the items and met back in the kitchen.

"First we put your hair in a *high* ponytail," Dad said.

Heidi hung her head upside down and gathered her hair into a ponytail on top of her head. She wrapped a ponytail tie around it.

"Perfect," Dad said. "Now have a seat."

He took the clean plastic soda bottle and cut the side of it. Then he tucked Heidi's ponytail inside the bottle and threaded the end of her ponytail through the opening at the top.

"Now I'm going to clip this plastic cup to the side of your hair." Dad fastened the cup with a clip. Then he placed the end of Heidi's ponytail inside the cup.

"Ta-da!" Dad exclaimed. "I give you the winner of Crazy Hat Day!"

Heidi raced over to the mirror and squealed. "I LOVE it!"

Then Henry ran into the kitchen and asked, "Love WHAT?"

Heidi turned so Henry could see her new look.

"Whoa!" he shouted. "I love it TOO!"

Heidi clapped her hands and did a little happy dance. *Wait until Smell-a-nie sees THIS!*

Chapter 5

WRONG DAY

Heidi made sure that she was the first one to arrive at the bus stop in the morning.

Henry had to run to catch up. He was wearing his favorite secret spy hat. They waited for the other kids to arrive.

As Bryce walked toward the waiting area, Heidi waved to her. Bryce had on a riding helmet. She stopped and stared at Heidi.

"HOW did you DO that?" Bryce asked.

Heidi shrugged. "It's a little trick I learned from my dad."

Bryce circled Heidi. "That has to be the coolest hat I've ever seen!"

Heidi beamed. "Thanks! Your hat is fun too."

Bryce patted her helmet. "Well, it's not as great as yours, but you know me. I LOVE horseback riding!"

Heidi nodded and looked around at the other kids who had begun to arrive.

She saw a chef's hat, a stocking cap, and a graduation cap. The craziest hat—besides hers—was a sombrero, which really wasn't very crazy.

But Heidi didn't mind standing out. She was getting tons of attention for her soda bottle hat. As she boarded the bus she heard:

"Hey, soda pop girl!"

"Nice hat, Heckelbeck!"

"That's SO-DA-mazing!"

"You're the queen of pop, Heidi!"

Heidi sat next to Bruce, like always. He had a cereal box on his head.

"I hope that's not full," said Heidi.

Bruce laughed. "Um, it was at first, and I kind of spilled cereal all over the floor at home. But that's the good thing about having a dog."

Heidi's eyes bugged out. "He ate everything that spilled?"

Bruce nodded. "EVERYTHING. It's like having an automatic vacuum cleaner!"

Heidi turned and faced forward. Maybe she could train her little brother to do that too.

At school Lucy greeted Heidi and Bruce at the bus. Lucy had on a homemade hat with one puffy cloud around the rim and a rainbow arching across the top of her head. Lucy and Heidi pointed at each other and squealed.

"I LOVE your hat!" Heidi cheered.

"No, I love yours MORE!" Lucy said.

Bruce stepped between the girls and pulled out a small handful of cereal. "Well, MINE'S the yummiest!" he said.

They all busted up laughing as they walked up the steps and into the school building.

Stanley ran up to Heidi and grabbed her by the arm. "Yours is the BEST hat I've seen yet!" he exclaimed.

He was wearing a shark hat with the jaws clamped around his head.

It looked like the shark was about to take a big bite out of Stanley!

"Thanks!" Heidi said. "And your hat is totally terrifying!"

Stanley shrugged. "I mean, it's from a store," he said. "I wish I'd made one like you did! It's great!"

Then he waved bye and dove back into the stream of kids going to class.

Principal Pennypacker passed by.

"Are you a POP star?" he asked.

Heidi laughed, but then she did a double take when she saw that the principal had on a wizard's hat. A *real* one. Heidi would have to ask him about *that* later.

Then somebody bumped Heidi, and she almost fell over. Of course it was Melanie. She had on a pink cowgirl hat with rhinestones all over it.

"So that's your hat?" was all Melanie said. "It's pretty cool."

Heidi's eyes widened. "Thanks, Melanie."

But then the pink cowgirl hat dipped down as Melanie added, "Well, except for ONE thing."

Heidi took a deep breath and braced herself for what was coming next.

"You wore it on the WRONG day," Melanie said. "That's NOT a crazy hat. It's crazy HAIR." Then she skipped away as usual.

Now Heidi wanted to scream. She stomped her foot and said, "Merg! No matter what I do, Melanie ALWAYS has to win."

Lucy rested her hand on Heidi's shoulder. "Only if you LET her win. Now let's get to class before you get fizzy."

Chapter 6

A WACKY TACKY IDEA

After school Heidi ran to her bedroom and slammed the door. She unclipped the cup on the side of her head and freed her hair from the soda bottle. Then she flopped onto her bed and buried her face in her pillow.

"Heidi?" It was her mom.

The door squeaked open and closed. Heidi felt the mattress bend as her mom sat on the bed. "Do you want to tell me what happened?"

Heidi sighed and rolled onto her side. "You know my crazy hat? Well, it was TOO crazy!"

Mom tilted her head to one side. "But isn't that what you wanted?"

Heidi propped herself up. "Yes, but then everybody wore REGULAR hats. It made me stick out like an elephant on a trapeze. And to make matters worse, Melanie said my hat was a crazy hairdo, NOT a crazy hat."

Heidi flopped back down on her pillow.

Mom sighed. "Well, it really doesn't matter what Melanie thinks," she said.

"She'll always say the opposite of what you want to hear. And it's definitely not your job to *please* her either—or anyone else, for that matter."

Heidi rolled back over. "I know," she mumbled. "But she just makes me SO mad."

Mom nodded. "I understand."

Then Heidi yawned. "Tomorrow is Wacky Tacky Day," she said. "But I'm not even going to try." She yawned again and snuggled into her pillow. In no time at all, she fell asleep.

When Heidi woke from her nap, it was almost dinnertime. She padded downstairs, rubbing her eyes.

When she got to the kitchen, she saw Lucy and Bruce sitting at the table—eating tacos!

"Wait, am I dreaming?" Heidi said, pinching her arm.

Mom set a plate of tacos at Heidi's seat and waved her over.

"Your mom called us over so we could plan our outfits for Wacky Tacky Day with you!" Lucy said.

Bruce nodded. "And she had a really awesome idea!"

Heidi heard a loud clatter and turned to see Mom rolling an old trunk up to the table.

"Behold!" Mom said, running a hand along the top of the trunk, like it was a fabulous prize. "This trunk has my clothes from when I was *your* age. And everything in here is guaranteed to be wacky, tacky, and *totally* outdated."

Lucy and Bruce watched Heidi to see what she thought.

Heidi scratched her head and thought for a moment.

Maybe if they all dressed tacky *together*, then it wouldn't be so bad.

"Okay, I'm in," she said.

"YAY!" Lucy and Bruce shouted at the same time.

After dinner the kids tried on everything in the trunk.

"Wow, you sure dressed weird back then!" Heidi said.

Mom swiped Heidi with a rainbow leg warmer. "Yes, but remember, yesterday's fashion is today's wacky tacky!"

Then the three best friends modeled their wild outfits for Heidi's family.

Chapter 7

QUEEN OF TACKY!

Heidi's mom drove the wacky tacky threesome to school in the morning. As the car inched slowly toward the drop-off area, Heidi saw the other outfits. Kids wore frumpy grandma dresses, big bow ties—one kid even had the tallest platform shoes ever.

Mom pulled up to the curb.

"Ready, my fellow wackadoodles?"
Heidi called out as she grabbed the
door handle.

"Ready!" Lucy and Bruce cried.

They opened the door and hopped

onto the sidewalk. Heads began to turn.

"Look at THEM!" cried Stanley, pointing.

Heidi, Lucy, and Bruce stood side by side in a silly pose. Heidi had on a headband with floppy flower antennae. She wore a dark pink tutu and mismatched shoes on her feet—a high top and a rubber boot.

Lucy stood with her hands on her hips. She had on a dress with a flower-print shirt and mismatched leggings. Around her waist she wore *two* belts.

Bruce stood like a pretzel rod. He had on plaid shorts, a bow tie, and a life-size fish necklace. He topped off his look with a googly-eyed, fang-faced ball cap.

Nobody looked wackier or tackier than Heidi, Lucy, and Bruce—that is, until Principal Pennypacker twirled across the playground. He had on a pair of grown-up footie pajamas with panda bears on them!

He tippy-toed and spun all the way
up the stairs to the entrance. Then
he stopped and waved to Heidi and
her friends.

"Love your outfits!" he called. Then he extended one leg behind him and pointed his toes. He hopped through the door on his other foot. Heidi and her friends cheered loudly. Nobody had more school spirit than Principal Pennypacker.

Later in the classroom, Heidi almost fell out of her chair when she saw Melanie. She had *not* dressed up at all!

Melanie took one look at Heidi and covered her mouth to hide her laughter. "Wow, Heidi, I always KNEW you were wacky tacky, but this outfit is the wacky tackiest!"

Before Heidi could say anything, Melanie flipped her hair and continued. "You won this school spirit day by a mile, Heidi Heckelbeck. But that's only because I chose NOT to dress up. You want to know why?"

Heidi rolled her eyes. *No,* she thought.

Melanie's smile dropped. "Because there is NOTHING cool about looking tacky. And, by the way, it kind of looks like you're trying too hard to stand out."

Heidi folded her arms. "That's the whole entire point," she shot back.

Then Mrs. Welli, who was wearing a patchwork skirt and flowered shirt, asked the class to quiet down. Melanie raised her hand, and Mrs. Welli called on her.

"I have a special announcement," Melanie began. "As everyone knows, being tacky is really NOT my thing at all, unlike some people in this class. But stay tuned tomorrow for my winning superhero costume. Oh, and congratulations on being the Queen of Tackiness, Heidi! It's SO YOU."

Heidi sank down low in her chair and muttered under her breath, "Winning superhero costume, huh? We'll see what the *Book of Spells* has to say about THAT!"

Chapter 8

SPELL POWER

That night Heidi was upset. Luckily, Henry made her laugh with a story about getting his funky scarf caught in the toilet at school.

After dinner Heidi slipped her *Book of Spells* out. She found a superhero spell and read it over.

Finding the Superhero Within

Have you ever had to deal with a villain? Then perhaps you may have wished you had a superpower to handle the villain? Well, search no further! If you'd like to unlock your inner superhero, then this is the spell for you!

Ingredients:

1 page from your diary

1 piece of felt

1 brand-new Band-Aid

1 glass of milk

Gather the ingredients and mix them together in a bowl. Hold your Witches of Westwick medallion in one hand and use your other to cover the mix. Chant the following words:

ALAKAZAM! AND ALAKAZOO!

BRING FORTH THE POWER

THAT'S SUPER IN YOU!

Heidi gathered the ingredients in a mixing bowl and stirred them together. She held her medallion in one hand and covered the mix with the other. Then she chanted the spell.

Heidi waited for the magic to work. But the only thing she felt was tired.

I'll get ready for bed now, she thought. *Then the spell can take hold while I'm sleeping.*

Heidi put on her pajamas, brushed her teeth, washed her face, and climbed into bed. As she drifted off to sleep she wondered what her superpower would be. *Maybe I'll be able to FLY? Or what if I'm able to talk to animals and help missing pets find their way home. . . .*

Chapter 9

SUPER HEiDi

Heidi's eyes blinked open. *Today I get to find out my SUPERPOWER!* She threw back her covers and leaped out of bed with her arms spread out like a bird.

Thwump! She crash-landed on her carpet.

"Guess I can't fly." Then she hopped up and ran to her mirror.

"Hmm, what if my superpower is INVISIBILITY?" Heidi squeezed her eyes shut and tried to disappear. When she opened her eyes, there she was, staring back at herself in the mirror.

"Maybe breakfast will help," she said to herself. She hurried downstairs to the kitchen and poured a bowl of cereal.

Then, when no one was looking, Heidi reached down and grabbed the leg of the kitchen table and tried to lift it. *Ooomph!*

The table wouldn't budge.

Heidi began to think her superhero spell was a *super* dud. She trudged back to her room to get dressed. When she opened her closet, she jumped back. Hanging up was a *real* superhero suit.

Heidi pulled it down and laid the suit on her bed. It had a shimmery blue bodice with a gold letter *H* on the front. It also had sparkly red belt and a red satin cape with gold trim. It even came with a black eye mask and long black gloves.

Heidi quickly changed into her costume. Then she looked at herself in the mirror and squealed.

"Look out, Melanie!" she cried. "SUPER HEIDI is here to save the day!"

Chapter 10

SUPER DAY

On Thursday, the Brewster Elementary playground looked like a superhero fashion show.

Bruce was dressed as Atom Boy. He had Styrofoam balls sticking out on all sides of his costume. Heidi noticed some of his atoms were falling off.

103

She ran over to pick them up, and she stuck them back onto his costume.

Bruce sighed. "You're a lifesaver, Heidi. Usually my inventions hold up better than this."

Heidi stuck one more ball onto his suit. "You just needed someone to fasten the ones on the back!"

They high-fived.

Across the playground, Heidi saw
Lucy. She wore a purple leotard,
lavender tights, and a lavender cape
that was definitely dragging on the
ground.

Lucy stumbled on it, and Heidi zoomed over, faster than fast, to help her friend.

"Are you okay?" Heidi asked.

"Yeah, I'm fine," Lucy said. "I keep tripping over this silly cape. I don't know what's going on. It fit perfectly when I tried it on last night."

Heidi inspected Lucy's superhero outfit.

"Here!" she said. "The stitching has come undone."

Lucy hung her head. "Now I'm doomed to trip and fall ALL day!"

Hmm, Heidi thought. "I've got an idea. To the art room!"

Once there, Heidi found a pair of scissors. "Would you like me to trim the bottom of your cape so you won't trip over it?"

Lucy clapped her hands. "I would LOVE that!" she said.

Heidi measured and carefully cut a little bit of the bottom off Lucy's cape.

Lucy danced around when Heidi was done. "It's perfect, Heidi! You're my hero!"

Suddenly, Principal Pennypacker knocked on the art room door. "Hello, girls," he said in a high-pitched voice that didn't sound like him at all. And it wasn't him! It was Melanie. She was dressed up exactly like Principal Pennypacker!

Heidi cupped both of her hands over her mouth. "Wow, Melanie!" she exclaimed. "That truly is the perfect superhero idea!"

Melanie patted her bald wig, which had tufts of hair on either side. "Thanks," she said. "I love YOUR costume too."

The girls smiled at each other— *real* smiles.

A warm feeling whooshed over Heidi, and all at once she knew what her inner superpower was. And she wasn't going to let it go to waste.

She continued to help people all day long. She fed the class guinea pig.

She watered the class plants. She
even stacked the chairs at the end of
the day.

"Thank you, Heidi. You're the most kind and helpful student I have!" Mrs. Welli said. "To return the favor, I would like to donate a dollar for every lap you finish tomorrow at the Fund Run."

Heidi beamed. She thanked Mrs. Welli and then skipped all the way to the bus. This had been a wild, wacky week for Super Heidi, but she had learned an important lesson. It only takes kindness to shine a light through the darkness. And Heidi felt brighter than ever.

Check out the next book starring **HEiDi HECKELBECK**

Heidi Heckelbeck was the busiest girl on the planet. Dad called her Lil' Miss Busy Bee.

On Monday, Heidi had swim practice with her team, the Little Mermaids. They worked on the butterfly stroke.

On Tuesday, she had Young Rembrandts. It was an after-school

An excerpt from *Heidi Heckelbeck Takes the Cake*

art class with Mr. Doodlebee. The class had been working on a giant aquarium collage. Heidi made a pink neon jellyfish from paper plates, paint, and yarn.

On Wednesday, Aunt Trudy took Heidi to the Fine Arts Museum. They got to see all kinds of original art, from paintings to sculptures to videos to stuff that Heidi couldn't describe.

Heidi's math tutor came over on Thursday—that's because Heidi needed help with word problems, especially the ones with fractions.

And, of course, Friday night was

An excerpt from *Heidi Heckelbeck Takes the Cake*

Movie Night at the Heckelbeck house. They watched Henry's favorite movie for the fifth time. Not that Heidi was counting.

Saturday morning was all about the swim meet. The Little Mermaids crushed the Aqua Maidens in free-style and breaststroke.

Then, on Saturday afternoon, Heidi discovered she had accidentally booked two playdates for the same day!